COASTER

Paula Kluth

Illustrations by Vinsensiana Aprilia

ISBN: 9781690179092

Edited by Carrie Jones
Cover design by David Miles
Book design by David Miles & Teresa Bonaddio

Printed in the United States

Coaster was a remarkable puppy.

He had a fine, black coat with brown spots the color of milk chocolate.

His ears were very floppy. One sometimes pointed up and one usually pointed down.

His nose was wet and just the right amount of shiny.

wet and just-the-right-
amount-of-shiny nose

floppy ears

fine, black coat

The thing that made Coaster so remarkable, however, was not his fine coat or his floppy ears or his wet and shiny nose.

He was remarkable because he had

WHEELS.

Shiny wheels.

Spin-y wheels.

Super-speedy wheels.

Slightly squeaky wheels.

They were amazing. He was amazing.

Coaster lived in an animal shelter.
Everyone there loved his wheels.

He was
admired by
all of the other
puppies . . .

and even some of the kittens.

Each day,
Coaster napped
in his cage,

chewed on
his toys,

and barked
along with the
other puppies.

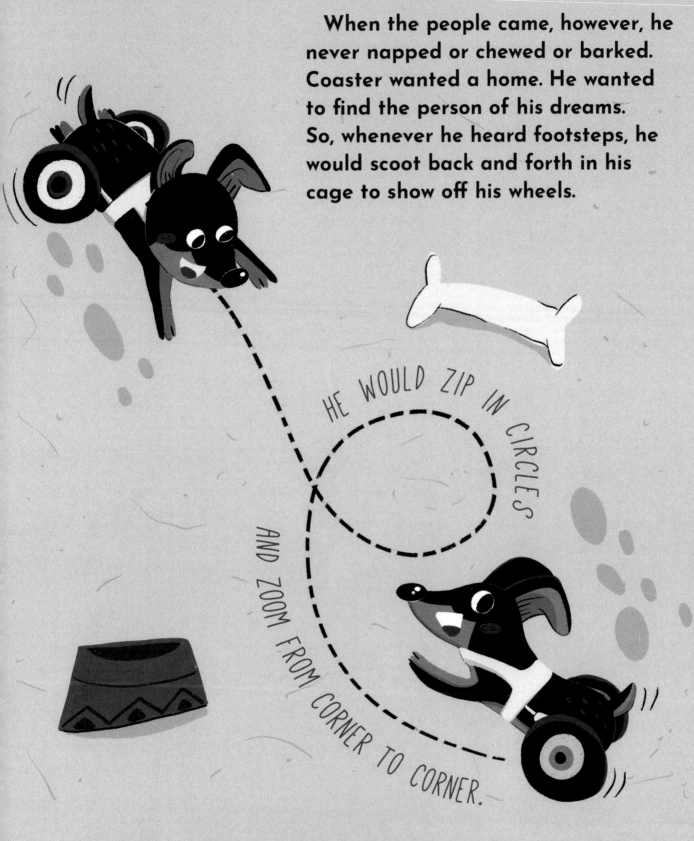

When the people came, however, he never napped or chewed or barked. Coaster wanted a home. He wanted to find the person of his dreams. So, whenever he heard footsteps, he would scoot back and forth in his cage to show off his wheels.

HE WOULD ZIP IN CIRCLES

AND ZOOM FROM CORNER TO CORNER.

His silver spokes would spin. His tires would turn, and he would careen across the concrete with a *whirrrrr*.

All of the puppies (and some of the kittens) stared in awe.

"Coaster is amazing," they thought. "He has a fine coat, floppy ears, and a shiny nose, but best of all, he has wheels."

The other puppies could not zip and
zoom around their cages. All they could
do was jump up and down and yip and
yap and yowl.

They dreamed of having wheels so that they could scoot and spin like Coaster. They dreamed of having wheels so that they too could be

AMAZING.

All of the puppies felt sure that Coaster would be the first to find a home, but he was not adopted during his first week at the shelter.

Many people came, but they did not choose Coaster. A man visited and picked the puppy in the cage next to Coaster's.

That puppy didn't zoom or scoot. She just chewed on a stuffed bunny all day. The man didn't seem to mind. He liked her and took her home.

Then, the puppy across from Coaster was picked. He didn't zoom or scoot either. He just stretched and yawned and slept a lot, but a lady passed by him and thought he looked sweet. She took him home.

Day after day, new people arrived. The cages would open. The puppies would tumble out panting with excitement. Each one would be carried out in loving arms.

Many people stood by Coaster's cage. They watched his tricks. Some of them clapped with enthusiasm when Coaster scooted in circles. Others giggled with appreciation when he zipped and zoomed. Every now and then, someone offered Coaster pats and scratches or even a treat.

Nobody, however, opened his cage to take him home.

Coaster was so confused. "I'm such a good dog," he thought. "I have a fine coat, floppy ears, and a shiny nose, and best of all, I have these wheels. My wheels are amazing. I am amazing."

Days passed.
Coaster stopped
looking forward to
the footsteps, the
people, and the
visits.

One day when the people
came, he napped instead of
scooting, zooming, spinning,
and whirrrrring.

That night,
he dreamed
he had found his

PERFECT
PERSON.

The next morning, Coaster awoke and saw someone sitting right in front of his cage.
He blinked.
He could not believe his eyes.
This person was looking at him and smiling.
She was different from the others. She was remarkable. In fact, she was

PERFECT.

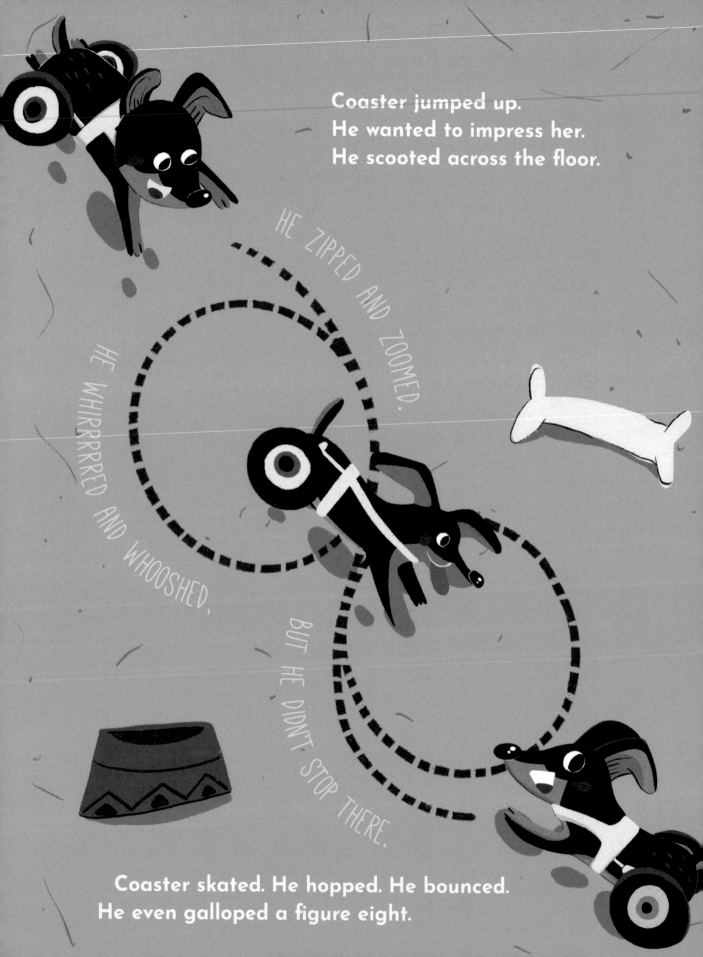

Coaster jumped up.
He wanted to impress her.
He scooted across the floor.

HE ZIPPED AND ZOOMED.

HE WHIRRRRED AND WHOOSHED,

BUT HE DIDN'T STOP THERE.

Coaster skated. He hopped. He bounced.
He even galloped a figure eight.

The person did not clap or giggle or even feed him a treat. She just kept smiling at Coaster. Then, she whispered his name, nodded, and pointed into his cage. Coaster's tail began to wag and then shake and then it waggled so hard that his wheels began to shudder and clank and sing.

Big hands scooped Coaster off the floor and placed him in the loving arms of the person. She hugged him tight.
Coaster nuzzled and licked her neck. He trembled with joy.
Even though it took a very long time to find his person, he knew he got

THE VERY BEST ONE.

He knew, in fact, that he was the luckiest dog in the shelter. So, he tried not to look too excited as he passed the other puppies (and some of the kittens) in their cages.

He tried not to smile too widely with his eyes or stand up too proudly on his front legs, but he could not help himself, because Coaster wasn't just leaving the shelter.

He was leaving with
a zip,
a zoom,
and a whirrrrr,
and on wheels even grander
and more amazing than his own.